Tell Me Your
Best Thing

Tell Me Your Best Thing

by Anna Grossnickle Hines

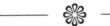

illustrated by Karen Ritz

DUTTON CHILDREN'S BOOKS   NEW YORK

Library of Congress Cataloging-in-Publication Data

Hines, Anna Grossnickle.
    Tell me your best thing / by Anna Grossnickle Hines;
illustrated by Karen Ritz. — 1st ed.
        p.   cm.
    Summary: Eight-year-old Sophie reluctantly joins the new
club formed by Charlotte, the class bully, and finds herself
being hurt when her best friend is manipulated into telling
Sophie's darkest secret.
    ISBN 0-525-44734-2
    [1. Clubs—Fiction. 2. Bullies—Fiction. 3. Friendship—
Fiction.] I. Ritz, Karen, ill. II. Title.
PZ7.H572Te   1991   91-7833
[Fic]—dc20   CIP
                                                   AC
Published in the United States by
Dutton Children's Books,
a division of Penguin Books USA Inc.

Printed in U.S.A.   First Edition   10 9 8 7 6 5 4 3 2 1

For all the Charlottes
who helped me get it right
A.C.H.

For Natalie
and her Nativity School friends
K.R.

Contents

Tell Me Your Best Thing

The Invitation

"Come on, you guys. We're going to start a club," Charlotte called. Sophie's stomach did a little dip. She and Jill had just decided to play dodge ball during their morning recess.

"What kind of club?" Jill asked.

"I'll tell you when I get everybody all together," Charlotte said.

"Want to?" Jill asked, turning eagerly to Sophie. Her dark curls bounced, and she had that grin that showed the little gap between her two front teeth.

Sophie bit the corner of her lower lip and shrugged. She figured Jill's eagerness *wasn't* for dodge ball.

"We're going to get a drink of water first," Jill told Charlotte.

"Well, hurry up, okay? We'll meet in the corner by the tree."

Sophie's stomach dipped again. That was the same corner where she'd gotten her hands caught in the fence in second grade. That had been one of Charlotte's games, too.

Sophie frowned as she watched Charlotte dash across the playground. She hadn't had any problems with Charlotte so far in third grade, if you didn't count the summer. But that was just the trouble. With Charlotte, you never knew when it might happen.

Dragging the toe of her sneaker along a crack in the blacktop, Sophie lagged behind her friend. When Jill stopped, Sophie nearly bumped into her.

"Don't you want to be in the club?" Jill asked.

Sophie shook her head, making her straight brown hair bounce against her cheeks. Then she remembered Jill's eager look and shrugged again. "I sort of do and sort of don't."

"How come?"

"It's just that, well, Charlotte's ideas always sound good to start with, but . . ." Sophie sucked in a deep breath and let it out in a long sigh. "For me they don't always end up that way."

Jill nodded. "You mean like last year when we played pilgrim-in-the-stocks?"

"That was one time," said Sophie. "Remember? Ms. Baker had to get the custodian to bend the fence and get my hands unstuck. All the kids crowded around to watch, and I felt stupid. But Charlotte thought it was funny."

"Yeah," Jill agreed. "She was laughing her head off. You should have told her to stuff it."

Sophie chuckled. That was one thing she liked about Jill. She had what Sophie's mother called spunk. Charlotte *never* got the best of Jill.

"How about if we join the club?" Jill suggested. "And if she starts to do anything, you know, mean, I'll just tell her to knock it off."

Jill tucked a springy curl behind her ear, but it bounced right out again. Even Jill's hair is spunky, Sophie thought. Her own hung straight, just about even with her chin. She blew her bangs up with a puff, but they fell back down. Wimpy. Like herself.

"Okay," Sophie agreed after a pause. She needed some spunk on her side, even if it was borrowed.

They each took a quick sip at the drinking fountain, then scurried toward the tree.

"Hurry up," Charlotte called as they ran up. "You're the last ones."

The Club

Sophie saw that Charlotte had collected five kids. Meghan was at her elbow. Hannah and three boys clustered around them. Counting Charlotte, Sophie and Jill would make eight.

"Okay, now we've got everybody," Charlotte announced, "so here's my idea. This is going to be called the Best-Worst Club. If you want to be in, you have to tell your best thing and your worst thing."

"You mean like, who's your best friend?"

Jill asked. She tossed an arm across Sophie's shoulder. Sophie grinned.

"Noooo," Charlotte moaned, flashing Jill a don't-be-stupid look. "What I mean is, if you want to be in this club, you have to tell the *best* thing that ever happened to you and the *worst* thing that ever happened to you."

Sophie got that flippy feeling in her stomach again.

"The best thing that ever happened to you?" Josh crinkled his face.

"Yes," Charlotte said.

"Like what?" asked Josh.

"Like getting picked to play Gretel in our class play," Charlotte said. "That could be my best thing." She pointed her finger as she spoke. Everything about Charlotte was pointy. Her fingers. Her eyebrows. Even her hair slicked into a tight ponytail high on the back of her head. She looked

kind of like a skinny banana, in Sophie's opinion.

Josh punched Bobby with his elbow. "Was your best thing getting picked to play Hansel?"

"No way!" Bobby said.

"My best thing was hitting that home run last summer when the score was tied," Kevin said. "Last game of the season and we won!"

Josh slapped him on the back, and all three boys started jumping and cheering.

"We won the game! We won the game! Hooray for Kevin 'cause we won the game!"

Uh-oh, Sophie thought. Here they go.

"Stop it! You can't act like that in this club," Charlotte ordered. "We can't talk when you're yelling."

"So what!" said Josh. "We don't want to be in your stupid club anyway! Come on, guys. Race you to the tires."

"No big loss!" Charlotte shouted after them.

Sophie resisted an impulse to follow. Oh, well. At least she had Jill this time.

"We don't need them," Charlotte declared. "This will be a girl's club. Now, we all have to tell our best thing. I'll go first because it's my idea."

"But you already said your best thing was getting picked to be Gretel," said Jill.

"No, I didn't. I just said that *could* be my best thing, but it's not. In this club you have to tell your really truly best thing, or it doesn't count."

"Do you have to tell your really truly worst thing, too?" asked Sophie. She tucked her lower lip between her teeth.

"Of course you do," Charlotte said. "Otherwise it wouldn't be fair."

Sophie wasn't sure what fairness had to do with it. She also wasn't sure she wanted to tell Charlotte her really truly worst thing, club or no club. But it was kind of late to try to get out of it now.

"So my best thing, my very, very, *very* best thing," Charlotte went on, "was winning the art contest and having my picture put in Mrs. Starr's office."

"Yes, and I won second place," said Jill.

"But you didn't get your picture in the principal's office," Charlotte said smugly.

Jill wrinkled her nose and drooped her eyelids, imitating Charlotte's snooty look. Sophie saw, but Charlotte missed it.

"Okay, Sophie. You go next. Tell us your best thing."

Sophie bit her lip again. It was hard to think so fast. She had never won anything or gotten picked to be the most important person in a play. Maybe flying up to see her grandparents last summer was her best thing. Of course! That was it. Not the trip, but something that happened on the trip. Sophie smiled.

"My best thing," she said, "was last summer, on my eighth birthday, when my grandma gave me her doll. She got it for her birthday when she was just the same age as me."

"It must be *old*," said Charlotte, curling her upper lip as if something smelled bad.

"She *is* old," Sophie defended meekly. "That's why she's special." She should have known Charlotte would think old was yucky.

"I've seen the doll she's talking about," said Jill. "She's really beautiful."

"She has a satin dress and a red velvet cape with white fur all around the edge," Sophie said. "And a hat with a big, long feather."

"She sounds neat," said Hannah. "Can I see her sometime?"

"Sure. Anytime you want."

"Me, too?" Meghan asked.

"Maybe I can bring her to school sometime," Sophie suggested. "Then you could all see her."

"Good," said Charlotte. "Now who's next? Jill, you go next, then Hannah, then Meghan."

Jill took a deep breath. "I think it was the time my mom came in after we'd gone to bed and said we could get up to watch *The Sound of Music* on television. She made chocolate pudding. We ate it while it was still warm, and we all snuggled up together under a cozy blanket. We stayed up really late."

"I get to stay up late all the time," said Charlotte.

"Me, too," said Hannah, "but what Jill said sounds more special."

Sophie thought so, too, and was glad Hannah had said so.

"Now you, Hannah," said Charlotte.

"My best thing was when my daddy took me to Disneyland. I hadn't seen him for a long, long time. But then, the summer before last he came and took me, just the two of us. We rode on everything together, and he promised that it wouldn't be so long until he saw me again."

Hannah's smile faded. "He was wrong about that. I guess that's my worst thing."

"What is?" asked Jill.

"That he broke his promise. That the last time I saw him." Hannah's eyes glistened behind her glasses. She blinked and forced a trying-to-be-cheerful smile.

The other girls were silent for a moment. Sophie tried to imagine not seeing her dad for over a year. She felt as if there were a big sponge in her chest, sucking her in.

"Okay, Meghan. It's your turn," Charlotte directed.

Meghan grinned as the others turned to her. She was round-cheeked and rosy with bushy red hair that made a halo all around her head. If Charlotte was a banana, Sophie thought, then Meghan was a peach. Sometimes she wondered why Meghan liked Charlotte so much. They were nearly always together.

Maybe some people wondered why Jill liked Sophie so much. She and Jill had lots of fun together, especially making things. Last Saturday they had made a whole new room for Jill's mouse house, with lace curtains and everything. That had been Sophie's idea. Sophie pulled herself back from remembering to listen to Meghan's best thing.

"It was when we came home after a regular, ordinary day and my mother had fixed an extra special dinner," she said. "Like a birthday, only it was for everybody. We even had presents on our plates. All of us, my sister and my stepdad and me. For no reason."

"No reason?" Sophie asked. Sometimes they celebrated half-birthdays in her family, with half a cake and just a little present. But they had never had a celebration with presents for no reason at all.

"My mother said she just wanted to let us all know that she loved us," Meghan said.

"That is special," said Hannah.

"Now the worst things," said Charlotte. Sophie stiffened. But at that very minute, the bell rang.

"Oh rats!" said Charlotte. "We'll have to tell worst things at lunch recess. Everybody meet right here as soon as you finish eating. Okay?"

Sophie sighed. At least she had until lunchtime to try to figure out what to do.

Private Talk

"This way," Sophie said as Jill picked up her lunch tray. Sophie led her friend away from the group of girls already seated at a table.

"Don't you want to eat with Charlotte and the others?" Jill asked.

Sophie shook her head. "Come on. Before they see us." She settled on a spot near the center of the room, close to a pillar which hid them from the other girls' view.

"I have to talk to you," Sophie said as

she and Jill scooted their legs under the table. "Alone."

Jill poked her straw into her milk carton. "What about?"

"About the club," Sophie said.

"What about it? Don't you like it?"

"I like the best things part, but I don't know about the worst things. My worst thing is about Charlotte." Sophie watched as Jill dipped a Tater Tot in a puddle of catsup. "Do you like her?"

"Sometimes I do and sometimes I don't," said Jill. "She has good ideas, but she's too bossy."

"*And* she hurts people's feelings." Sophie took a bite of green Jell-O and squished it with her tongue before she swallowed it. She was thinking that Charlotte not only hurt people's feelings. She hurt them and then laughed about it. Sophie winced re-membering. "You know last summer when I went to Brownie camp?"

"Yeah. I couldn't go because we went on vacation."

"Well, something happened at camp that I never told you," Sophie said. "I never talked about it to anybody."

"How come?"

"Because I wished it never happened."

"What?"

"Well, I . . . I took Elpha. You know, my elephant?"

Jill nodded.

Sophie glanced around to make sure no one was listening. "I hid her in the bottom of my sleeping bag so no one would know and say I was a baby or anything. But then Charlotte felt the lump and she got Elpha out and started saying stupid stuff in baby talk. 'Sophie has a BeeBee. Did you bring your blankee, too?' You know, stuff like that."

"You should have bopped her," said Jill.

"Then she and Meghan started tossing Elpha around in the tent. Every time I'd

try to grab her back, they'd throw her, like playing keep away. Charlotte ran out of the tent with her, and a bunch of other girls joined in.

"They were running all around between the tents and in the bushes and everything. When the leaders came out to see what was going on, nobody had Elpha. Meghan's mom asked everybody, one by one, but they all said they didn't have her and they didn't know where she was.

"So then Meghan's mom said it was time to go to bed and we'd all look in the morning. I wanted to go look with my flashlight, but she wouldn't let me.

"In the tent Charlotte and Meghan kept giggling all night long. And I kept worrying that Elpha was out in the bushes."

Sophie hoped Jill wouldn't guess the part of the story that was too embarrassing to tell even a best friend. She also hoped that Charlotte and Meghan's giggles had kept them from hearing her own sniffles. She had tried so hard not to cry.

"Did you ever find her?" asked Jill.

"I sure did! The next morning, at the top of the flagpole, hanging by her ear!"

"Oh! Poor Elpha!" Jill exclaimed.

"Yes, poor Elpha. And pretty soon everybody in the whole camp was cracking up. Even the big girls in the camp way past ours could see *my* stuffed elephant hanging up there.

"Then Charlotte got everybody started saying the stupid baby stuff again. 'Oh, poor Sophie. Did she lose her li'l elphalent?' She had that smirky look, you know, like this." Sophie forced her mouth into a wide grin, squinched her eyes, and raised her eyebrows.

Jill chuckled. "That's just how she does it! You should have looked right back at her like that."

"Yeah," Sophie sighed. That *is* what Jill would have done. Sophie wished she were that brave. She never seemed to be able to think fast enough to do anything back to Charlotte. Besides, she was afraid it would just make things worse.

"At least you got Elpha back," said Jill.

"It is kind of funny. An elephant on a flagpole."

"Maybe if it isn't *your* elephant!" Sophie protested. "I hate it when a whole bunch of people look at me. Even if it's just because I have to give a book report in front of the class. And when all of them were saying baby talk at me, well, it was just my worst thing, that's all."

Jill's look softened.

"Now I'm afraid that Charlotte will say her stupid blankee jokes and make a big deal about it all over again," Sophie went on. That was the truth, even if it wasn't the whole truth.

"Maybe you could tell another worst thing," suggested Jill.

"It's supposed to be your really truly worst thing," said Sophie. "The only thing I can think of that even comes close was the time I got my hands stuck in the fence. And that was because of Charlotte, too. If I don't tell my really truly worst thing, Charlotte might, and *she* probably thinks it's the camp one."

And if Charlotte tells it, Sophie thought to herself, she might tell all of it, if she knew. Of course, she might anyway, but that was a risk Sophie figured she'd have to take. If any of it was to be told, Sophie would rather it be in her own words than Charlotte's.

Jill watched Sophie scrape her fork around in leftover catsup. "We could just not be in her club. I won't be in it if you don't want to."

"She'd want to know why and everything," said Sophie.

"Yeah. She'd make a big deal about it," agreed Jill. "Besides, I think the club might be fun. I like Hannah and Meghan."

Sophie set her fork carefully in the long slot on her tray and looked up at Jill. "I guess I'll just have to tell. And if she starts

saying that stupid thing, I'll just have to
. . . ignore it or something."

"Don't worry," said Jill. "If she does that,
I'll tell her to stuff a sock in it."

A slow grin spread across Sophie's face,
and her eyes twinkled. "No, not a sock.
Her blankee!"

Jill clapped a hand over her own mouth
to keep from spraying her last sip of milk
all over the table as both girls burst into
giggles.

Worst Things

"There you are," Charlotte said as Sophie and Jill joined the group of girls waiting under the tree. "We were looking all over for you."

"We wanted you to eat with us," added Hannah.

"Well, we're here now," said Jill.

"Yep," echoed Sophie. "We're ready." She hoped she really was.

"Then let's start," said Charlotte. "I'll be first again."

Josh, Kevin, Bobby, and Corky came trotting up. They were all linked together with their arms across one another's shoulders.

"Hey, guess what?" Josh shouted.

"You're a four-headed monster," Jill guessed.

"Funny, funny," said Josh. "But that's not it. Guess again."

"Maybe we don't want to," said Charlotte.

"Yes," said Meghan. "Maybe we're too busy."

"So who cares?" said Josh. "Because we have our own club. It's called the Stupid Jerk Club. To get in, you have to tell who's the stupidest jerk in the school."

"Yeah, duh, who could dat be?" said Corky, making his face and voice droop stupidly.

The boys guffawed.

"That's easy," declared Jill. "You are!"

"What you say is what you are," Bobby retorted.

"And you guys said it first," said Charlotte. She turned her back to them and extended her arms to make a little huddle with the other girls. "Come on, let's just ignore them."

"Come on, let's just ignore them," Josh said in a high, whiny voice. The boys ran off.

"Stupid jerks," said Jill. "That's the perfect name for their club."

"Okay, let's start," said Charlotte. She glanced around, making sure she had everyone's attention. "My worst thing was when I fell down and broke my arm. I had to go to the hospital and get it X-rayed and get a cast put on it and everything."

"I'll bet that hurt," said Hannah.

"You'd better believe it!" Charlotte exclaimed. "It hurt like anything, and afterwards, inside that stupid cast, my arm itched like crazy. I had to have it on for six weeks!"

"My worst thing was when I fell down on the ice and cut my chin," said Meghan. "I had to get eight stitches."

"I remember that," Sophie said. "It happened when we were in Ms. Baker's class. The ice was right over there."

"Oooh! Yeah, I remember, too," said Charlotte. "You were bleeding all over the front of your jacket."

Meghan winced. "The worst part of all was that Ms. Baker had just told us to get off the ice, and I *was* getting off. But then Corky slipped and grabbed hold of my arm. He didn't fall down but I did. Ms. Baker started yelling, 'Didn't I tell you to get off of there? See what happens when you don't do as you're told?' So I was hurt and in trouble at the same time. And it wasn't even my fault!"

Sophie knew she'd never been hurt that badly. She'd never had stitches or broken bones. But she tried hard to think of a time she'd been in trouble, hoping to come up with something worse than having her stuffed elephant kidnapped and hung on the flagpole.

The only thing she could remember was when her first-grade teacher tapped her on the head for shaking Larry Watson. He was letting himself be all limp like a rag doll, his head and arms flopping around. Emily and Kevin had giggled, so Sophie was giving Larry another good hard shake when Mrs. Grant suddenly appeared behind her. She tapped Sophie crisply and reminded them all that they were supposed to be planting their bean seeds. Somehow it didn't seem so bad now, but at the time, Sophie had worried that Mrs. Grant might send her to the principal's office. That's what happened to bad kids. She knew that even in first grade.

"Sophie next," Charlotte said.

Startled out of her thoughts, Sophie

gently bit her lower lip as she tried to find the words to begin. But Jill spoke first.

"Wait before you tell it, Sophie," she said. "I think we should have a rule in this club that nobody can make fun of anybody else's worst thing."

"Or their best thing either," added Hannah.

"Nobody's going to do that," said Charlotte.

"I think we should all promise," insisted Jill.

"I'm the one who started this club," said Charlotte, "so I'm the one who gets to make up the rules."

"Well, we're all in it," said Jill. "And if you want us to stay in it, then everybody should agree about the rules."

"We could vote on it," suggested Hannah.

"That's a good idea," said Meghan, twirling a finger in her hair.

"All right," said Charlotte in a huff. "Everybody who thinks we should have that rule raise your hand."

Four hands went up immediately. Charlotte added her own. "Okay, that's a rule. Now go ahead, Sophie."

"Wait," protested Jill. "We all have to promise."

"Cross my heart," said Hannah, tracing an X on her chest with her finger.

"Me, too." Meghan crossed her chest.

So did Jill and Sophie.

"Now you," Jill said to Charlotte.

"I voted for it, didn't I?"

"You have to cross your heart."

"Okay. Okay. Cross my heart." Charlotte huffed and waved a limp finger across her chest.

"Good. *Now* tell us your worst thing, Sophie," said Jill with a grin at her friend.

"Okay." Sophie took a deep breath. "It was in Brownie camp last summer when

my elephant got put up on the flagpole. I was embarrassed and I didn't know where she was all night."

"Oh, yeah, your poor li'l elphalent," Charlotte cooed.

"No making fun," Jill objected.

"I'm not," Charlotte defended. "It's just . . . well, it was funny!"

Jill fixed her gaze on Charlotte. "She doesn't want everybody in the whole school to know about it."

"So who's going to tell anybody that Sophie took her dumb old elephant to camp?" Charlotte retorted. "Who even cares? Go ahead and take your turn."

Elpha's not a dumb old elephant, Sophie thought, but she didn't say anything. She was too relieved to be out of the spotlight. She'd hardly had to tell anything at all. Not about her feelings at least, about how lonely she'd been sleeping without Elpha, or about the crying. Just the silly part about the flagpole.

Jill began. "I have two things, actually."

"You have to pick just one," insisted Charlotte. "Only one can be *the* worst thing."

"Don't worry. I will," Jill snapped. "I *was* going to say it was last year when I threw up in front of the whole class, but then I remembered something else. Something even worse than that." She paused dramatically. "My very worst thing was the day my mother dumped everything out of *all* my drawers and off *all* my shelves. When I got home from school, everything was in a big pile in the middle of my room. A huge pile! I had to put it away all by myself. It took me *four* days to do it, and I could only come out to eat and go to school!"

"Ooooh! Your mother must be mean," said Charlotte.

"No, she isn't!" Jill protested, shaking her head slightly so her dark curls bounced. "She was just mad that time. She's usually not like that."

"What was she mad about?" asked Meghan.

"Because I didn't put my things away right. She found some dirty clothes in with the clean ones. Some toys, too." Jill chuckled. "And an old, dried up peanut-butter sandwich."

"We're pretty lucky that all the bad things don't happen to just one person," said Hannah. "There are enough for everybody."

"I . . ." Sophie began, then glanced at Jill. "I think we should make one more promise. I think we should promise never to tell anybody else's best or worst things." It was risky to ask such a promise. It was risky to ask anything of Charlotte that wasn't her own idea. But Sophie wanted to

be as sure as possible that what had happened at camp would not come up again.

She was pleased when Charlotte not only
agreed, but added, "And never ever talk
about them except in this club. Let's
pledge with all our hands together. Like
this." She extended her right hand. One by
one, the other girls placed theirs on top of
hers.

"Now cross your heart and say, 'I promise never to tell any of the secrets of the
Best-Worst Club or to make fun of anything anybody ever says in the club.'"

Worse Than Worst

The tardy bell was ringing as Sophie entered the classroom the next morning. "I need to ask you something," she whispered as she hurried past Jill. She winced as she slipped into her seat, then glanced around hoping no one had noticed. Jill was the only one looking at her. Corky and Josh, who sat at the same group of desks, were busy making ugly faces at each other.

Sophie folded her left leg up under her so that she wasn't sitting flat on her bottom. That wasn't so bad.

Corky turned to show her the face he was making. His eyes were crossed, his lower lip twisted inside out, and he had his pinky fingers poked up his nostrils. It was gross. Sophie rolled her eyes at Jill, whose desk was kitty-corner to hers.

"Jerks," Jill whispered with a nod.

Josh heard her. He curled his upper lip and crossed his eyes. Jill turned away.

"Hey, you guys want to know what my worst thing is?" Josh asked. "It was when my little sister was born!"

"Ha! Yeah!" Corky burst out. "My worst thing was when my sister was born, too. And she's older than me!" He crowed and slapped his desk.

"My worst thing is having to sit in this group with two Stupid Jerks," said Jill.

Sophie agreed with that. Josh wasn't so bad all by himself, but Corky was always goofing off and causing a commotion. He made another gross face at her. She ignored him. He wasn't her biggest problem at that moment.

Mr. Cook asked the class to quiet down, and Sophie tried to concentrate on her spelling workbook. Her left foot had started to tingle, so she carefully switched to sitting on her right. Soon it went to sleep, and she had to change legs again.

"Sophie, I think you might be more comfortable if you would sit properly on your chair with both feet on the floor," Mr. Cook said.

Sophie slipped her leg out from under her, easing her bottom onto the chair. It was not more comfortable, but she wasn't about to say so. No way!

When the recess bell rang, Sophie grabbed Jill's hand and watched while Charlotte led Meghan and Hannah to their meeting place under the tree.

"Come on, this way. We have to be alone so I can ask you that question." Sophie pulled Jill to the far end of the building. "They didn't see us. They're still by the tree."

"So ask me now, before they come looking for us," Jill urged.

"Okay." Sophie hoped Jill would give her the answer she wanted to hear. Otherwise . . . she could have a very big problem. She took a deep breath and spit out her question. "Do you think after you've already told your worst thing, that you have to tell if you get a new worst thing?"

"I don't know," said Jill. "There's no rule."

"Do you think we could sort of make one, just the two of us, and not tell?" Sophie asked.

Jill shrugged. "I guess. Why? Do you have a new worst thing?"

"I don't want to tell it," Sophie whispered earnestly.

"What is it?"

"It's even more embarrassing than all that baby talk about Elpha and the flagpole and everything," Sophie said. "Charlotte could really make some good jokes about this."

"Then let's just make that rule," declared Jill, as if that settled it. "They won't even know. You can just tell me."

"And we won't say anything about the rule, right?" Sophie asked. "Because if we do, then they might wonder why we made the rule, and maybe they'll say we have to vote." She had wanted an ally, but now that she had one, she was a little worried that the whole thing might backfire.

"It's just between us." Jill crossed her heart and raised her right hand. "So tell me."

"You promise not to tell anybody?"

"I just did!"

"Oh. I thought that was just about the rule part, not the worst thing part."

Jill sighed. "Are we best friends or what?"

"I just had to be sure." She glanced around and lowered her voice. "You know that electric heater on the wall in our bathroom? The one with the coils inside that get all red?"

"Sure. Remember that time when I spent the night and we turned out the lights and pretended it was a campfire?"

"Yes, that's the one. Well, last night when I got out of the tub I was cold and, well, I sort of got too close to it. I, uh, I backed into it and burned myself."

"Ooh! Where?"

"You know."

"On your bottom?" Jill exclaimed. "You burned your bottom?"

"Yes. Shhh!"

"Ow! Does it hurt to sit down?"

"Of course! What do you think!"

Jill giggled.

"It's not funny!" Sophie insisted, but she let out a little giggle herself.

"It's a funny place to burn yourself."

"Yeah. You should see what it looks like. It has crisscross lines, like a waffle. I looked in my mom's big mirror."

"Like a waffle!" Jill blurted.

Sophie nodded, then swung around as Charlotte's voice pierced her ears.

"There you are!" Charlotte was running toward them, her ponytail swinging from side to side. She carried a small box in her hands and had Meghan and Hannah at her heels.

"We've been looking all over for you," Meghan called. "Why didn't you come to the club?"

Sophie's throat tightened. What could she say?

Fortunately, Jill had no problem. "Sophie was helping me study my spelling," she lied.

Charlotte looked from Jill to Sophie. "Well, next time you aren't coming, you have to tell us. Tell me, because I'm the leader. Okay?"

Sophie nodded. Thank goodness for Jill.

"Now you can all see what I made for the club. Look." Charlotte lifted the lid off her box to reveal five buttons. Each one had a large BW in the center. Underneath, the word *club* was written in smaller letters. Around the edge were tiny sad and happy faces.

"Oooh! Neat!" said Jill, taking a button from the box. "Did you really make these?"

"I drew them, and then my mom made them into buttons with her machine," Charlotte explained. "You know that one she always uses in the booth at the carnival."

"Wow, these are great!" said Sophie. She was happy to talk about anything but worst things.

Charlotte beamed. "The BW is for Best-Worst. Now we have something so everyone will know we're a real club."

"Yes," said Meghan. "Kind of like a symbol."

Sophie pinned her button on, feeling

slightly uneasy that she and Jill had made up a rule all by themselves. Charlotte wouldn't like it. But then, it was the only way to be sure Sophie's secret would stay secret. Just between her and Jill. Nobody else.

Jumping Beans

All five girls proudly wore BW buttons as they paraded back to class after recess. Sophie sat on the edge of her seat, leaning forward to keep most of her bottom off the chair. She sat that way as she worked her first two math problems. But it wasn't very comfortable. So she leaned way over to her right side for the next problem. And then to the left.

Jill grinned at her. Sophie grinned back and almost laughed again. All that came out was one snort.

Corky looked up. "Hwoink! Hwoink!"

Josh snickered.

Jill's face was buried in the crook of her arm. Sophie could tell that Jill had the giggles by the way her hair was jiggling. She pressed a hand tightly over her mouth to keep her own laughter from bubbling out, but when Jill peeked up at her, another snort escaped.

"Hwoink! Hwoink!" Corky repeated, to Josh's enjoyment.

Sophie stretched her mouth sideways with her fingers and stuck her tongue through the slit at Corky. Jill laughed out loud.

"Would you four care to share the joke with the rest of the class?" Mr. Cook asked.

Jill sat up straight and shook her head. Sophie straightened also, wincing at the pain caused by the quick change in position. She hoped Mr. Cook hadn't noticed. What if he thought she was making a face at him? She hated getting in trouble. If she wasn't careful, she'd have another new worst thing. At least his voice had scared all the giggles out of her.

When none of the students offered an answer to Mr. Cook's question, he said, "Then I suggest you concentrate on math."

Sophie took a deep breath. She put both hands on her chair and lifted herself off. That felt better, but she couldn't do any math that way. Well, maybe she could do the thinking part. Forty-eight plus twenty-nine. Okay, first eight plus nine. Eight plus nine. It was hard to think with her hands busy holding her up. And her arms were beginning to ache. Seventeen. That's right. Put down the seven and carry the ten. Lean to the left, lean to the right.

"Sophie, you seem to be having quite a problem sitting still today," said Mr. Cook. "Have you been eating jumping beans?"

Sophie shook her head and stared down at her math paper while the rest of the class giggled.

"That's enough," said Mr. Cook. "Let's get back to work."

Back to work. Corky made another stupid face, but Sophie ignored him. Twenty-six take away eighteen. Rats! Not enough ones on top. She'd have to regroup. She leaned forward on the edge of her chair.

Suddenly—*Crash!*—she was on the floor, on her bottom, and everyone was looking at her.

"Are you all right?" asked Mr. Cook.

Sophie nodded. She blinked hard. Her bottom hurt and her chin hurt. She'd hit it on the edge of the desk. And most of all, her pride hurt. But she couldn't let herself cry. She just couldn't. Not in front of everybody. And she certainly didn't want to tell her teacher about any of it. Keeping

her head down, she got carefully to her feet and picked up the chair.

"Since you are having such a problem sitting, maybe you'd like to stand up for the rest of the morning. You can work at that little table in the back," said Mr. Cook.

Silently, Sophie picked up her paper and pencil and walked to the back of the room. Mr. Cook thought she'd been fooling around. He thought she'd been bad. They all did. She heard Corky snicker. She could feel everyone looking at her. She didn't dare look back.

Not even at Jill. If she looked at Jill, she'd cry for sure.

But at least she didn't have to try to sit down now. Sophie started on the next math problem.

"Psst!"

She squeezed her eyes shut and tried to think about fifteen take away eight.

"Psst! Sophie?"

As she leaned over her work, Sophie's hair fell forward, covering her eyes on the sides. She brushed more hair forward to make a screen in front, too.

"Hey? Hey, Sophie!"

She gave in and looked up. Bobby was leaning way over, his grinning face as close as he could get it. "What have you been eating?" he whispered. "Dumping beans?

Get it? Dumping you on the floor?" Some kids chuckled.

Sophie made a face. Bobby was a Stupid Jerk, too. So what if he got mad? He deserved it. Uh-oh. Mr. Cook was watching her again. She wished she could have just stayed home.

Hooray for the Club!

"Does it hurt a lot?" Jill whispered. She was right behind Sophie in the lunch line.

"Sort of a lot."

"Why didn't you just stay home today?" asked Jill. "You get to stay home if you're sick. Your mother could write a note."

"Would you want your mother to write a note that said you burned your you-know-what?" Sophie shuddered at the thought of handing such a note to Mr. Cook. She could picture that funny little grin he got sometimes and felt her face flush just thinking about it. And then the note would go to the office. Sophie could imagine the office people passing it all around and chuckling. No, coming to school was the best solution.

"Besides," she continued, "hurt isn't sick. Sometimes you don't get to stay home if you're hurt. Like if you have a broken arm. Remember? Charlotte came to school. And Meghan came when she had those stitches."

"Maybe your mother could say you have waffle-bottom disease," Jill whispered, then giggled.

"Shhh!" Sophie said, but she couldn't help smiling. She looked around to make sure no one else had heard. The fourth graders behind her were engrossed in their own conversation, and the boys in front of Jill weren't paying any attention either.

"Anyway, I couldn't stay home," Sophie said quietly. "My mom has to go to work, so I'd have to go to Mrs. Jackson's, my old baby-sitter. I didn't want to do that because of Christy. You know, that blabbermouth in second grade? She goes to Mrs. Jackson's after school and if she found out, *everyone* would find out. For absolute sure. She's worse than Charlotte."

Jill groaned. "So did your mom do anything to . . . you know, make it feel better?"

"Of course! First she made me sit in a pan of ice water."

"Sit in it?" Jill snickered.

"It's not funny!" Sophie protested, giggling in spite of herself. "It felt pretty weird. Then she put on aloe so it will heal up fast. It hurt lots worse last night."

Jill nodded. "Well, I think you're brave. That must have really hurt when you fell, and you didn't even cry."

Sophie looked at her friend. It hadn't been bravery that kept her from crying. It had been total fear. Fear of all those eyes looking at her and all those kids laughing. Being brave about pain was easy. Being brave about those other things, well forget it.

Jill picked up her tray. "Want to sit with the rest of the club?"

"Well, not exactly *sit*," Sophie responded with a little grin. She got her tray and looked around.

The other three club members were waving at them and pointing to the places they were saving at one of the tables.

Sophie kneeled on the bench, then eased herself down.

"Are you all right?" asked Meghan.

Sophie nodded.

"I think Mr. Cook is mean to make you stand up," said Hannah.

"It's okay. I like it back there. Nobody can bother me. Only Bobby, and he's not as bad as Corky."

"Let's eat fast and try to get swings today," said Charlotte, stuffing a bite of mashed potatoes into her mouth.

"I don't really feel like swinging today," said Sophie.

"Neither do I," said Jill. "Let's play something where you have to stand up."

Sophie shot her a please-don't-give-it-away look.

"I have lots of energy," Jill said quickly. "I don't feel like any sit-down games."

"How about kickball?" Hannah suggested.

"Yeah, kickball!" said Jill.

"I hate kickball," Charlotte declared with a scowl. "Besides, if we do that it won't be just our club. We'll have to be on a team with a bunch of other kids."

"So?" said Jill. "Everyone will still know we're a club because of our buttons."

"Yes," said Sophie, anxious to smooth

things over. "Since you made us these neat buttons, everyone is going to know that, no matter what we do."

"We'll play on the swings tomorrow," said Jill.

Sophie's stomach flopped. Why did Jill say that? Her bottom might not get better that fast, even if her mom put a ton of aloe on it. Trying not to let anyone else see, she nudged Jill with her elbow.

"I mean, next week," Jill corrected herself. "*Next week,* we'll play on the swings for sure."

Charlotte looked suspiciously from Jill to Sophie. "Why next week? Why not tomorrow? Why not today?"

"We told you. We don't feel like it!" said Jill.

"Well, I do," said Charlotte.

Jill looked at Sophie. Sophie swallowed. Somehow, she had to make Charlotte give up. "Actually," she began, "I hurt my bottom when I tipped my chair over, so right now I just don't feel like sitting down." It wasn't such a big lie, Sophie thought. It would be worth it if it would convince Charlotte to drop the argument.

No such luck. Charlotte peered at her with those squinchy eyes. "It hurt that bad?"

Sophie nodded.

"So why didn't you cry?" Charlotte challenged.

Sophie sucked in a gulp of air and stood with her mouth open, hoping desperately that the right words would somehow spill out. Only the words came from Jill.

"Because she's brave. Would you want to be a crybaby in front of the whole class?" Jill blurted. "We'll play on the swings next week. On Monday. That's only three more days. Okay, everybody? Let's make a promise."

"Why not tomorrow?" Charlotte squinted

at Sophie again, pushing her pointy face close.

"I might not be better by tomorrow," Sophie stammered. "I . . . I landed really hard." She breathed in quick little gulps. Charlotte seemed to be sucking up all the air. Sophie drew back but Charlotte pressed closer.

"I think you just want to have everything your own way," Charlotte snapped. Her eyes locked on Sophie's.

Sophie stared back at Charlotte. She could hardly breathe, let alone speak. What would she say if she were really brave, and not just about pain? If she had spunk, like Jill?

"Well, how about if *you* swing and we'll play kickball?" suggested Hannah.

Charlotte turned and Sophie took a step back.

"Yeah," Jill agreed. "We'll just do different things."

"I think we should all play together," said Meghan, leaning close to Charlotte, "because we're a club and everything."

"And I'm the one who thought of it, remember?" said Charlotte. "*And* I made the buttons."

"Yes, and it was a good idea," said Hannah, "so let's not fight. We're all in the Best-Worst Club together."

Hannah's smart, thought Sophie. She's trying to keep Charlotte happy.

"Yeah," Jill echoed. "We're all in the club."

"Hooray for the club!" Meghan patted Charlotte on the back.

Sophie watched nervously as Charlotte looked from Meghan, to Hannah, to Jill, and then . . .

"Hooray for Charlotte!" Sophie burst out as Charlotte's pouting eyes turned toward her. She forced a smile and secretly crossed her fingers.

"Come on, team!" whooped Jill. "Let's go!"

And like it or not, a sulking Charlotte was swept along as the little group headed for the kickball field. Sophie was careful to stay out of Charlotte's way.

The game was girls against boys, and near the end of the playtime, Charlotte scored a run on Meghan's kick. Slithering back to the girls' lineup, Charlotte paused and pinned her dark eyes on Sophie. Sophie watched Jill go to the plate to kick. Charlotte had caught her alone. Sophie twisted her fingers, keeping her eyes on the field. Charlotte moved closer, and closer still. Sophie felt the air being sucked away again.

"So," Charlotte challenged, "if you just hurt your rear end when you fell off your chair, how come you were having so much trouble sitting down before that?"

"I wasn't," Sophie lied. "I'm just nervous

. . . I mean hyper. I ate too much sugar for breakfast." Her heart fluttered. She watched Jill, pretending to be absorbed in the game.

Jill kicked and ran to first base. Relieved to escape, Sophie hurried to the plate. Meghan had stopped on second, so there were two on base.

Sophie kicked a good one. Both Meghan and Jill ran all the way to home plate. Kevin stopped Sophie on second, but her kick had scored two runs, even if she did have a sore bottom. She waved happily at the cheering girls.

As she watched Charlotte greet Meghan and Jill at the end of the line, Sophie's anxiety returned. Charlotte made a prissy face at Sophie, flipping her ponytail as she turned toward Meghan. Then Meghan put her nose in the air, too, and they both seemed to be arguing with Jill. Jill shook her head at them, then pulled them a step away from the end of the line, and the three made a little huddle. First Meghan, then Charlotte glanced curiously in Sophie's direction.

Watching them, Sophie shifted from one foot to the other. She wasn't paying attention when Hannah kicked the ball. Hannah was on her way to second before Sophie started to run for third. She barely made it.

In the line, the three girls were still talking. From third base, Sophie could hear their hushed voices but not what they were saying. Jill smiled and waved.

Uh-oh! Gina's kick! Sophie ran. Fast! She stepped on home plate just seconds before Bobby caught the ball . . . and the bell rang.

"We won!" Hannah shouted. "Seven to six!"

"Hooray for the girls!" Charlotte cheered, clapping Sophie on the back.

"So what," said Josh. "You only won by one point. Last time we beat you ten to three. Tomorrow we'll beat you a hundred to nothing, because you're not the Best-Worst Club! You're just the plain old Worst Club!"

"Liver-worst Club!" shouted Corky. "Ugh!"

"Very funny," muttered Sophie. Actually, she kind of liked liverwurst. The five members of the Best-Worst Club skipped back to class, hand in hand, in a wide line across the playground: Hannah, Sophie, Jill, Charlotte, and Meghan. And Sophie didn't even think about the fact that Charlotte was no longer sulking.

More Trouble

Sophie went directly to the back of the room.

"You may go back to your seat now, Sophie," said Mr. Cook.

She opened her mouth to ask if she couldn't please stay there, but seeing all the faces looking at her, Sophie closed it again. She picked up her pencil and shuffled toward her desk. If she could think of the right words, maybe she could ask him privately. She could say . . .

"Sophie really needs to stand up, Mr. Cook. She might wiggle again."

Sophie jumped at the sound of her name. It was Charlotte who had spoken! Sophie looked at her curiously, a creepy feeling sliding up her backbone.

"I think she can handle it," said Mr. Cook.

"No, you don't understand," said Charlotte. "She—"

"She has ants in her pants," Corky interrupted.

The whole class cracked up. All except Sophie and Jill. Jill was glaring at Charlotte.

Sophie's mind raced. Back to Charlotte's accusation at lunchtime that Sophie just wanted to have everything her own way. Back to the kickball game and Charlotte's insistent questions about why Sophie couldn't sit down. And then that mysterious huddle. Could Jill have . . . ?

"She does not! She just has . . . she has a sore behind," blurted Charlotte.

Jill was frantically signaling Charlotte to be quiet. Sophie's mouth dropped open. It was true. Charlotte knew! Jill had told her! Sophie peered at Jill, and the anxious look in Jill's round eyes confirmed it.

On the other side of the room, Meghan was whispering to Hannah. They knew, too. The whole club.

Sophie's insides burned. How could Jill dare to tell her secret? Especially after she *promised* not to. And she told *Charlotte* of all people!

"What's the matter? Did you get a whipping?" jeered Corky. "I'll bet that's it. I'll bet her dad took his belt to her."

"That is *enough!*" said Mr. Cook. "If Sophie has a problem, it is her own business. Not ours."

He walked to Sophie's desk and said quietly, "You may stand in the back if you prefer."

Sophie shook her head. Her throat felt so tight she couldn't speak. If she tried to say something, she would squeak. Besides, what could she say? Now she'd sit on her bottom no matter how much it hurt.

"Well, I'll leave it up to you," Mr. Cook

whispered. He gave her a puzzled look, then returned to the front of the room and asked everyone to take out their science books.

Sophie glued her eyes to the book, mostly to keep from looking anyplace else. But the words squiggled on the page. Reading was impossible. Even thinking about science was impossible.

She could only think about Jill. About how Jill had told Charlotte. How could she have done that? Jill was her best friend. Her very, very best friend. And she had promised.

Friend or Snitch?

When the bell rang for afternoon recess, Sophie hurried to the girls' rest room. Jill ran after her and grabbed her arm, but Sophie glared at her and pulled away. She was never going to speak to Jill again. Ever!

"I had to tell her," Jill whispered. "She said she was going to kick you out of the club because you're just a spoiled brat who has to get your own way."

Sophie shifted her gaze to the floor. If she were speaking to Jill, she could tell her who the spoiled brat was. Charlotte, that's who. Charlotte was the one who had just gotten her own way, and Jill had helped her do it.

The little green tiles on the floor were all lined up, square after square. I should never have trusted her, Sophie thought. I should have kept my secret to myself, all to myself in my own little square.

"I had to tell. I couldn't let her say those things about you. You're my best friend."

Some best friend, Sophie thought angrily. Couldn't even keep a promise.

"I had to." Jill was insistent.

Sophie couldn't hold out any longer. "Charlotte is the one who's a spoiled brat! She's the one who always gets her own way, and *you* helped her! Did you have to tell her the truth?"

"I couldn't think of anything else," said Jill.

"You could have said . . . you could have

said I got a shot or something. Everybody gets those." Now why hadn't she thought of that before? It was the perfect excuse. If she'd said that to Charlotte herself, maybe Charlotte would have dropped it and Jill wouldn't have . . . but it was too late now.

"Now everybody's going to know," Sophie said. "By the end of recess, I'll bet." A thud against the heavy rest-room door made her jump. "Somebody's coming!" She ducked into a stall. "Go wash your hands or something."

"They'll see your feet!" Jill whispered.

Sophie climbed onto the toilet, keeping her head bent so it didn't stick up over the top. She heard water splashing into one of the sinks.

"Come on, Charlotte. Just tell me." Sophie recognized Emily's voice. "I won't tell anybody. I promise."

"We can't tell you unless you're in the club," Charlotte said. "Right, Meghan?"

"Well, I want to join. I've got a good best thing. See, I can wiggle my ears. I learned it from my Uncle Bill."

"We'll have to have a meeting. After you join, then maybe we can tell you," Charlotte said.

Great, Sophie thought. Just as she had predicted. Everyone would know by the end of recess.

"No, we can't," said Jill. "It's Sophie's secret. It should be up to her."

"Well, where is she?" asked Charlotte.

Sophie caught her breath and held it. Would Jill betray her again? Wouldn't Charlotte just love to catch her standing on a toilet seat!

"How should I know?" Jill retorted.

Sophie breathed again, very quietly.

"It must have been her father who whipped her," Emily said. "I don't think my mother could spank that hard. Did he use a belt?"

"Nobody whipped her," Meghan said.

"Then what happened?" Emily pleaded. "Just tell me what happened. I'm going to join the club as soon as you have a meeting."

"We can't have a meeting until we find Sophie," Jill said. "And we *can't* tell her secret."

"Well, *you* told me," Charlotte said.

"That was a mistake," said Jill. "And it was just because you were saying things about Sophie that weren't true."

A bad mistake, Sophie thought, but at least Jill was sticking up for her now.

"Well, Emily is saying Sophie got a whipping. *That's* not true. I'm sure Sophie doesn't want everyone to think she got a whipping. Right, Meghan?"

Sophie pictured Meghan nodding, probably twisting a strand of that red hair. Charlotte could always count on Meghan to be on her side.

Charlotte went on talking. "It's better if she knows the truth. And she won't tell. She's going to be in the club. Right?"

"Right."

Even though they weren't face to face, Sophie had that feeling again that Charlotte was sucking up all her air. She put one hand on the wall to steady herself, crossed the fingers on her other one, and silently pleaded, "Don't tell! Don't tell!"

"Okay, I'll tell you," Charlotte said, "but you have to promise to keep it a secret."

"No!" Jill snapped. The word echoed off the tiled walls.

"She's going to be in the club," Charlotte said. "*You* told everybody else in the club, so *I* can tell Emily."

"*I* was trying to help Sophie. You're just trying to make yourself feel big! And Emily isn't even in the club anyway!"

"Let her tell her worst thing first," said Meghan. "Then she'll be in."

"Good idea," agreed Charlotte.

Right, Sophie thought. Wonderful idea! Just let everybody in the whole world be in the club, and then she can tell them all!

"Okay. Let's see," Emily said. "Um . . . I guess my worst thing was in kindergarten when Kevin kissed me because I was the other side of the bridge in London Bridge Is Falling Down."

"Okay?" asked Charlotte. By the snooty sound in her voice, Sophie knew exactly what Charlotte's face looked like, pointy eyebrows, squinty eyes, and all. She copied it. She wished she could do that where Charlotte could see it, nose to nose. But it was easy to be brave and think spunky things in the privacy of the rest-room stall.

"Okay," said Meghan.

Sophie waited for Jill to argue again, but she didn't. The door squeaked on the next stall, and Sophie saw Jill's shoes step inside. Fine time for Jill to lose her spunk . . . but it was probably a losing battle anyway. It was lost the minute Jill told Charlotte. Or maybe even before that.

"Well," Charlotte reported, "she burned her *bee-hind* on the heater."

"On the heater?" Emily asked.

"In the bathroom," Charlotte explained. "It made a waffle print on her rear end."

"Yeeow!" Emily exclaimed. "No wonder she doesn't want to sit down! Does she have blisters?"

"I don't know! I didn't see it," Charlotte scoffed.

Muffled giggles and shuffling feet moved toward the exit, and in a few seconds the rest room was quiet.

The door on the next stall squeaked again, and Jill whispered, "Sophie? It's all clear."

Sophie jumped down and opened her door. She felt all limp, like a deflated balloon. Too bad Jill, or somebody, hadn't been able to let all the air out of Charlotte.

"I'm sorry. I tried to stop her."

Sophie sighed. "I know. I heard you." She wished she could completely forgive Jill, but she just couldn't.

"Sophie?"

"What?"

"*Do* you have blisters?"

Sophie grimaced as she pushed the restroom door open. "No. Just red marks." Why hadn't she just kept her own mouth shut in the first place!

The Biggest Trouble Yet

"Where were you?" Charlotte asked Sophie as the class filed in at the end of recess. "We were looking all over for you."

"Some more girls joined the Best-Worst Club," Meghan said. "We have to have a meeting so they can tell you their best and worst things."

Jill looked at Sophie. Sophie looked at the floor.

"Maybe tomorrow," said Jill.

Maybe never, Sophie thought. That's

what Jill should have said. What was wrong with her anyway? Was she turning into a wimp?

As Sophie slipped carefully into her seat, Corky turned around and said loudly, "Hey, aren't the letters on your button backwards? Instead of BW, it should be WB for waffle butt!"

All around her, kids roared with laughter.

Josh slapped his desk. "Waffle butt! Waffle butt! Hey, waffle butt, do you want to sit in some syrup?"

Sophie stared straight ahead. Stupid jerk! Jerks and secret-tellers all around her. And all of them looking at her!

Suddenly the laughter stopped. Mr. Cook had entered and given them the look that meant "Quiet! Now!" He held the expression as he scanned each section. The room was still. A pencil rolled off someone's desk and stayed on the floor. No one dared to move.

Mr. Cook walked to Sophie's desk and handed her a pink slip of paper. Leaning down close to her ear, he whispered, "Mrs. Starr would like to talk with you, Sophie. You may go to her office now."

Sophie's eyes widened. You weren't sent to Mrs. Starr's office unless you did something really bad.

"It's all right," Mr. Cook said in a soothing tone. "She just wants to talk to you."

Sophie didn't feel all right. As she got up to leave, she thought she heard twitters of laughter.

Mrs. Starr wanted to see her. Sophie wished she'd stayed home. A note might have been embarrassing but nothing like this. So what if Mr. Cook had read it, and the grown-ups in the office had found it amusing? None of them would have teased her the way the kids had. Mrs. Jacobs, the school secretary, was her friend. Ever since kindergarten. She might have smiled a little, but she wouldn't have laughed. And she wouldn't have told the whole school.

In the office Sophie handed her pink slip to Mrs. Jacobs without a word.

"No smiles today?" Mrs. Jacobs asked.

Sophie shook her head.

"Oh, this must be serious business. Well, have a seat. Mrs. Starr will see you in a minute."

An older boy came in and handed some papers to the secretary. Sophie thought he was probably a sixth grader. On his way out, the boy grinned down at her. It wasn't a friendly grin. It said, "You're in trouble and you're going to get it."

Sophie slumped down and squeezed the arms of the chair. In trouble for what? What had she done that was bad?

Mrs. Jacobs had said it would just be a

minute. A minute was taking a long time. Sophie wished Mrs. Starr would hurry up and call her.

Now my worst thing is getting sent to the principal's office, Sophie thought.

Why did Charlotte have to go and start such a stupid club anyway? Why did Sophie have to join it? Ever since then, she'd been getting more and more worst things. First she burned her bottom. Then she knocked her chair over and got in trouble. Then her best friend told her secret to a bossy blabbermouth. Then the whole class found out, and the boys started calling her names. And now here she was, waiting for Mrs. Starr to . . . to do whatever the principal did to you when you were bad. Worse and worse and worse than worst. Sophie felt like there wasn't any best left. She felt like there'd never be another best thing in her whole life.

"Sophie!" Mrs. Starr said her name as if

she was surprised and very happy to see her. "Thank you for coming to see me. Come on in."

Mrs. Starr held her office door open, and Sophie stepped warily inside. The principal was being awfully friendly to someone in trouble.

The winning drawings from each grade were still on the wall. Sophie recognized Charlotte's. She had an urge to stick her tongue out at it. If she'd been alone, she would have.

"Sit down, dear." Mrs. Starr smiled and pointed to a chair. She sat opposite her. "I just want to have a little chat with you."

Sophie eased herself down. Mrs. Starr seemed to be very interested in the way Sophie seated herself.

"How are you, Sophie?"

"Fine."

"How are things at home?"

"Fine."

"You know, Sophie, you can tell me anything. If there is something bothering you,
if you are having a problem at home or at
school, you can always come and tell me. I
can help you work it out."

Sophie stared at her.

"Isn't there anything you want to tell me?" Mrs. Starr asked.

Sophie shook her head. Was this some kind of funny test? In class she usually knew the answers on tests, but she didn't have any idea what kind of answers Mrs. Starr wanted.

"Is anyone hurting you or being mean to you?"

"Oh, yeah." Sophie breathed a big sigh of relief. She finally knew the answer to one of Mrs. Starr's questions. "Some kids are . . . sort of."

"Here at school? In your class?" Mrs. Starr asked.

Sophie nodded, then squirmed uneasily. She hoped the principal wouldn't ask her to name names. She didn't want to be a snitch. That would only make things worse . . . if that was possible.

"What do these kids do?"

"Well, they just tease me." Sophie didn't

want to make it sound too bad, or Mrs. Starr would surely want to know *who.*

"Oh? What do they tease you about?"

"Umm," Sophie stalled. She'd have to be careful. "First they kept saying that I got a whipping, and then they called me, well, they called me something like waffle bottom, but they said a word that's not nice."

"Why would they say things like that?"

"Because it hurts when I sit down."

"Why does it hurt, dear?"

Sophie cast her eyes down. The carpet had blue flecks. Mrs. Starr was going to think she was pretty stupid, but Sophie had to answer the question. There wasn't any way to avoid it. Keeping her eyes on the carpet, she muttered, "Because I burned my bottom on the heater."

"What, dear?"

Sophie heaved a giant sigh and repeated more clearly, "I burned my bottom on the heater."

"Really?" Mrs. Starr seemed very surprised. "Nobody hit or spanked you?"

Sophie shook her head. "I just backed up too close to the heater after my bath."

Now Mrs. Starr sighed and smiled. "Oh, I see. Does it hurt very much, dear?"

"Only when I sit down," Sophie said.

"Oooh," Mrs. Starr crooned. "That must make it very difficult to be in school. Maybe it would be a good idea if you went home early today. Will your mother be there?"

Sophie shook her head. "Sh-she works. I stay by myself for just one hour until she gets home."

"Oh, I see. So you don't have a sitter then?"

Sophie shook her head again. Mrs. Starr didn't need to know she *could* have a sitter, did she? That was only for emergencies, and Sophie certainly didn't want to deal with that blabbermouth second grader at Mrs. Jackson's on top of everything that had already happened today.

"Well, it is close to the end of the day. How would you like to be Mrs. Jacobs' errand girl for the rest of the afternoon? That way, you won't have to sit down anymore today."

With a shy smile, Sophie nodded. "And those kids won't be able to make the whole class laugh at me either."

"That's true," said Mrs. Starr. "We've solved both problems for today, haven't we?"

Sophie wished she hadn't said the "for today" part because that made her start thinking: What about tomorrow?

Don't Be a Dope

The next morning Sophie marched up the sidewalk with long determined strides. Her mother had said she could go to Mrs. Jackson's if she wanted to, but her bottom didn't feel so bad. Sophie had decided she'd rather go to school and hear what people were saying about her than sit around with a bunch of babies and worry.

"I'll be brave," she had told herself as she pinned on her BW button. "I'll be spunky and brave the way Jill used to be before she started doing everything Charlotte says. I'll be the bravest person in the Best-Worst Club."

But her footsteps slowed as she neared the school grounds and saw the group of girls waiting beside the gate. Jill waved eagerly. Sophie lifted her arm, but let it flop. She was sorry to see Jill with Charlotte and Meghan. If Jill were mad at Charlotte, then *maybe* Sophie could forgive her former best friend. She and Jill could be brave together and tell Charlotte to mind her own beeswax. But it looked like Sophie would have to be brave alone. Even if she was, Charlotte wasn't the first person she wanted to meet this morning.

Charlotte obviously didn't feel the same way. She pushed her way to the front of the group. "How did you get to be errand girl yesterday?" she called out. "I thought you were going to get in trouble."

Sophie stared past Charlotte, trying to ignore her. She pinched her lips together and kept walking.

"She thought you were going to get suspended," said Meghan. She and Charlotte chuckled. So did Emily and Gina.

"She wouldn't get suspended!" Jill scolded. "She didn't do anything wrong!"

"Well, *la-di-da*," said Charlotte.

Sophie brushed past them. She wasn't feeling so brave after all.

"What's the matter with you, errand girl?" sneered Charlotte. "Are you too good to play with us now?"

"Shut up!" Jill ordered. "Leave her alone."

Sophie kept walking, past Jill and Hannah. There was Jill's spunk, defending her again. Why couldn't she do it herself? Just turn around, look Charlotte in the eye, and say, "Leave me alone!" Just like that. Just like Jill. But she couldn't. She could only

keep walking. Walking and getting more and more embarrassed.

"Well, so what! We don't want to play with you either, waffle butt!" Charlotte laughed shrilly.

"I said leave her alone!"

Sophie glanced around to see Jill clench her fists and push her face close to Charlotte's.

"Are you her bodyguard or something?"

"What of it?"

"Nothing of it. Nothing at all." Charlotte smirked and turned to the others. "It's just too bad she can't stand up for herself. Come on, you guys. Let's go play on the *swings.* Meghan, Emily, and Gina followed her, leaving Hannah and Jill alone at the gate.

Suddenly Sophie felt hot all over. Jill was a true friend, a good spunky friend, and she was the wimp. The wimp who couldn't even say one "Leave me alone" for herself.

Jill looked at her, but Sophie couldn't look back. She turned and continued across the school yard.

"Sophie, wait!" Jill and Hannah called.

As their footsteps neared, the hot feeling behind Sophie's eyes spilled into tears. She ran as fast as she could and ducked into the girl's rest room. As Jill and Hannah burst through the door behind her, Sophie locked herself into a stall. She struggled to keep her sobs quiet.

"Come on, Soph," pleaded Jill. "Charlotte's just a brat."

"Don't let her bother you," added Hannah. "We're your friends."

"Go away," Sophie choked out.

"Come on, Sophie, please?"

The rest-room door opened, and a teacher poked her head inside. "What's the problem here?"

"Nothing," said Jill.

"Then you'd better get back to the playground," the teacher ordered. "This is not a play area."

Jill and Hannah moved toward the door. "We'll wait for you outside, Sophie," Jill called.

The shock of almost being caught by a teacher had stopped Sophie's sobs. She pulled some tissue from the dispenser and blew her nose. She took several deep breaths, then slowly opened the door and stepped out.

The sight of her red, blotchy face in the mirror almost made her cry again. But she thought of Jill with her nose in Charlotte's face and stopped herself. "Don't be a dope, dope," she said out loud, then smiled weakly at her little joke. She splashed some cold water on her face and patted it with a paper towel.

She wished she'd had some water to splash in Charlotte's face. All of their faces. Whenever they started saying those dumb things, *Splat!* She'd let them have it! Let them laugh at that! She took off her Best-Worst button and threw it in the trash. It clanged against the side of the can.

Sophie sighed. *"Now,* I'm brave," she said. "In here, all by myself, where it doesn't do me one bit of good." The bell rang. That big loud sound seemed to be vibrating right inside her stomach. If she was going to be brave, Sophie told herself, she'd have to do a lot better job of it. She'd have to be brave out there, face to face with that bully Charlotte. Out there in front of everyone. But what could . . . ?

Suddenly, Sophie knew just what she could do. Quickly, she retrieved the button from the bottom of the trash can and slipped it into her pocket.

Being Brave

Sophie was the last one to enter the classroom, but she walked with her head up. Even when she knew everyone was looking at her. Even when she saw Charlotte's snooty look out of the corner of her eye.

As Sophie slipped into her seat, Corky whispered, "Waffle butt."

Sophie ignored him. I am very brave, she told herself, and he is a dope. That last part made her feel a little better. The corners of her mouth even turned up a teensy bit. Waffle bottom, she thought. It *is* pretty funny.

But her mouth tightened again at the sound of snickering from the area near Charlotte's desk. Sophie kept her eyes straight ahead. She had to wait until the time was right to do what she had to do. And then they'd see who had spunk. She'd show them. Charlotte, Meghan . . . all of them. Even Jill would see that Sophie could stand up for herself.

She was tempted to look at Jill now, but she couldn't. Not yet. So she didn't glance that way, not once during the whole reading period. And not even when Mr. Cook dismissed them for recess. Sophie put her books away and walked out the door without looking at anyone.

She walked so quickly that she almost bumped into Mrs. Starr.

"Sophie! Are you feeling better today, dear?"

Sophie nodded. It was true. Somehow she did feel better. And not just her bottom. She had a plan.

"You're able to sit down all right?"

Sophie nodded again.

"That's good," Mrs. Starr said, smiling brightly and patting Sophie's shoulder. Then she bustled off, leaving Sophie in the middle of the group that had gathered around them.

Charlotte grinned. It wasn't a nice grin. Sophie felt the air being sucked away again, but only for a moment. She sucked back, a good deep breath. The time was coming, and she wanted to be ready.

"That's goood! That's real gooood! Mrs. Starr's special pet feels better today," Charlotte crooned. "Isn't that nice, everybody?"

Jill stepped up to her. "Charlotte . . ."

she began, but Sophie grabbed her arm and pulled her back. This was her time, not Jill's. Charlotte was asking for it, and Sophie was going to be the one to give it to her. She had decided. Pushing Jill behind her, she faced Charlotte herself.

Charlotte huffed.

Sophie gulped, but she didn't back down. Pulling the BW button out of her pocket, she extended her hand. "Here," she said. "I don't want to be in your club anymore. I don't want to be in a club with anyone who tells other people's secrets and doesn't care how they feel."

"Fine." Charlotte snatched the button. "What about your friend, Jill? She told your secret first."

Jill opened her mouth, but Sophie interrupted her again. "She shouldn't have told, but at least she didn't tell the whole school. And she only told you to try to get

you to stop saying mean things about me. You want to know what my really truly worst thing is, Charlotte? My really truly worst thing is that I was ever in your old club!"

For once, Charlotte was speechless.

Sophie turned and stomped off. She didn't really know where she was going, but she ended up at the drinking fountain where she took long gulps of the cool water. Then she came up for air. Nice deep breaths filling up all the space in her chest.

She looked back at the group still gathered in front of the classroom. No one had followed her. Good. She'd rather be alone anyway. She didn't need the kind of friends who told secrets and hurt feelings. Not the kind of friends who did it on purpose and didn't even care.

Sophie sighed and leaned down for a second long drink. As she tasted the cool water, she heard the slap of running feet and then her name.

"Sophie! Sophie!"

She straightened and wiped the last drip from her chin.

"We gave our buttons back, too," Jill called.

"We didn't want to be in that club either," added Hannah. "Charlotte's too . . . you know."

"Mean," Sophie filled in.

"Sophie, I'm really sorry I told her your secret," said Jill.

Sophie shrugged. "I guess nobody can stand up to people like Charlotte all the time. Even somebody spunky, like you."

"That's why we have to stick together," Jill answered. "So we can help each other out."

A smile spread across Sophie's face as she looked at her best friend. "Yeah. I'm sorry I got mad."

"I don't blame you," said Jill. "I broke a promise."

"Sometimes you have to think about *why* somebody does something, though," said Sophie. "I mean, are they *trying* to be nice or really trying to be mean?"

"Do you think Charlotte will ever learn to be nice?" asked Hannah.

"Maybe if we all tell her to cut it out whenever she starts being mean and bossy, she could learn," said Sophie.

"Like you just did," said Hannah. "That was brave."

"Yeah," Jill agreed. "Real spunky!"

Sophie beamed. "I know. It's my new best thing."

Hines, Anna
Grossnickle

Tell me your best
thing

$13.95

DATE			

© THE BAKER & TAYLOR CO.